nickelodeon

TEENAGE MUTANT NINJA TURTLES™

D0053213

PIZZA PARTY!

illustrated by Patrick Spaziante

Based on the screenplay "Day One, Part One"
by Joshua Sternin and Jeffrey Ventimilia

Random House 🏠 New York

Four mutant turtles live
in the sewers
of New York City.

They are brothers.

They are ninjas.

Leo is the leader.

Raph likes to fight.

Donnie can build
anything.

Mikey is a joker.

7

The Turtles leave
the sewers
for the first time.

New York City is
dark and dirty.
The Turtles love it!

The Turtles see

a man on a scooter.

The man is afraid
of the giant Turtles.
He drops a box.

What is in the box?

It is pizza!

"Pizza is the best!"

says Mikey.

The Turtles hear

a scream.

Two men in blue
are grabbing
a girl!

Leo leads the attack!
Raph jumps into action!

Donnie swings his staff.

Pow!

The man falls
to the ground.

Mikey discovers that the men are really robots!

Small pink aliens are inside the robots! They are called the Kraang.

The Kraang escape!

The Turtles save the girl.

Her name is April O'Neil.

"I know how
we can celebrate,"
Mikey says.

Pizza party!

© Viacom International Inc.